THE BERENSTAINS' B BOOK

GROLIER
BOOK CLUB EDITION

THE BERENSTAINS' B BOOK

A Bright & Early Book

RANDOM HOUSE/NEW YORK

 Published in the United States by Random House, Inc., New York, and simultaneously in Canada by Random House of Canada Limited, Toronto. Trade Edition: ISBN: 0-394-82324-9. Library Edition: ISBN: 0-394-92324-3. Library of Congress Catalog Card Number: 78-158387. Manufactured in the United States of America.

W X 6 7 8 9

Big

brown

Big brown bear

Big brown bear,

blue bull

Big brown bear,

blue bull,

beautiful baboon

Big brown bear,

blue bull,

beautiful baboon

blowing bubbles...

Big brown bear, blue bull,
beautiful baboon
blowing bubbles
biking backward...

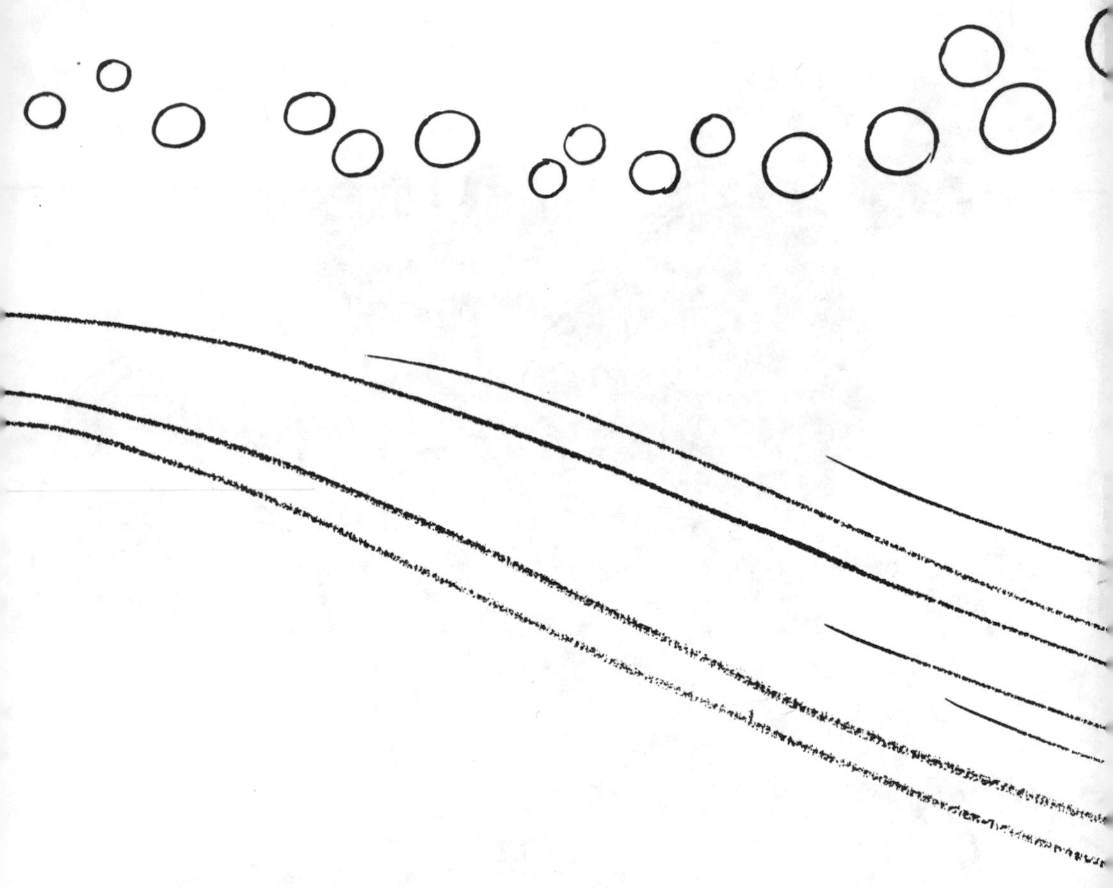

Big brown bear, blue bull,
beautiful baboon
blowing bubbles
biking backward,

bump...

B

M

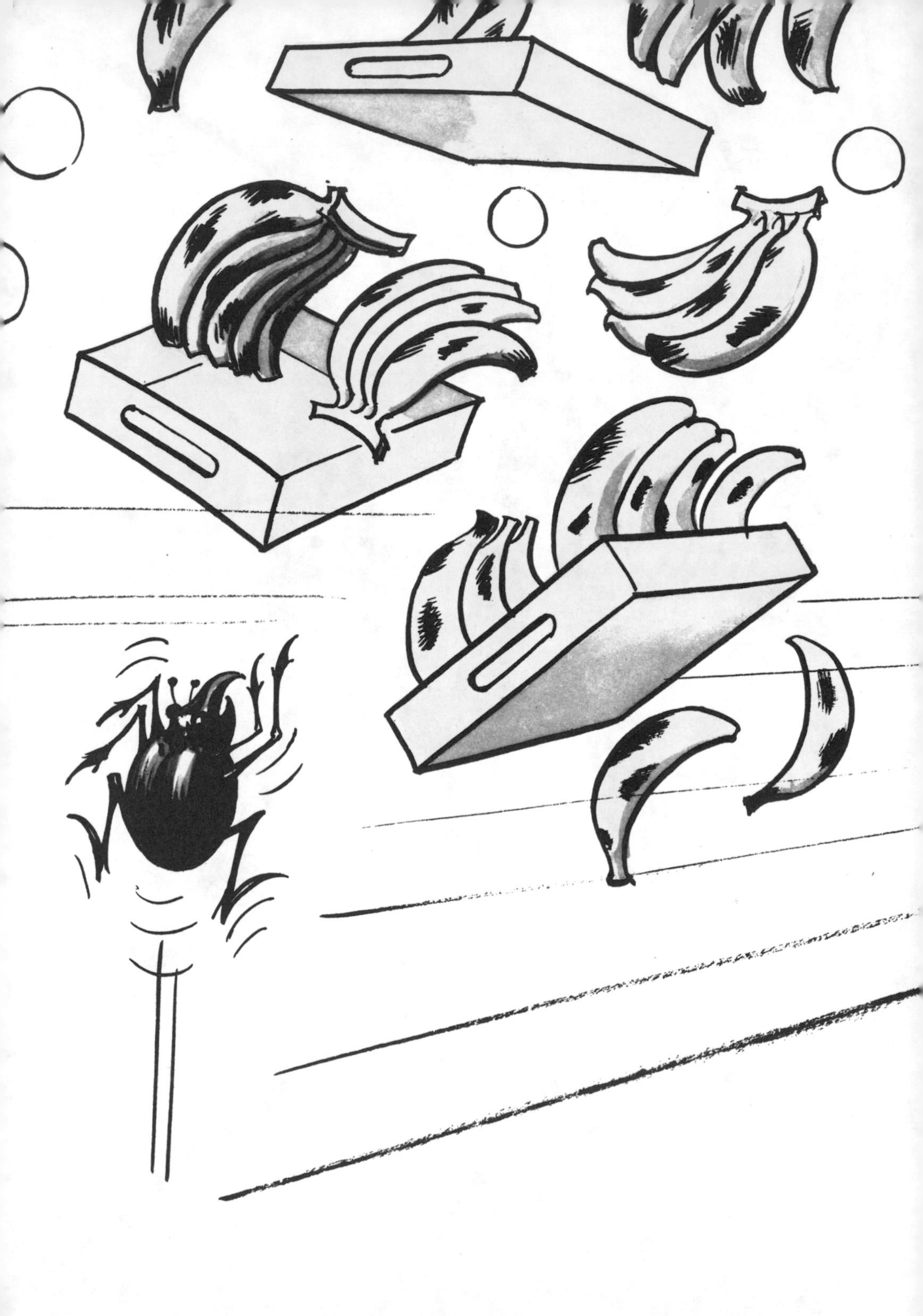

Big brown bear,
blue bull, beautiful baboon
blowing bubbles biking backward,
bump black bug's
banana boxes...

Big brown bear,
blue bull,
beautiful baboon
blowing bubbles
biking backward,
bump black bug's
banana boxes **and**
Billy Bunny's
breadbasket...

Big brown bear,
blue bull,
beautiful
baboon
blowing bubbles
biking backward,
bump
black bug's
banana boxes

and

Billy Bunny's
breadbasket

and...

Brother Bob's

baseball bus...

BOOM
BUSTER
BANJO
BUGLE
BOB'S

Big brown bear,
blue bull, beautiful baboon

blowing bubbles biking backward,
bump black bug's banana boxes **and**
Billy Bunny's breadbasket **and**
Brother Bob's baseball bus **and**
Buster Beagle's banjo-
bagpipe-bugle band...

and

that's

what...

BEAGLES
BAGPIPE
BAND

broke Baby Bird's balloon.